All children have
a strong desire to read
to themselves...

*and a sense of achievement when they can do so.
The* **read it yourself** *series has been devised to
satisfy their desire, and to give them that sense
of achievement. The series is graded for specific
reading ages, using simple vocabulary and
sentence structure, and the illustrations
complement the text so that the words and
pictures together form an integrated whole.*

LADYBIRD BOOKS, INC.
Lewiston, Maine 04240 U.S.A.
© LADYBIRD BOOKS LTD MCMLXXVII
Loughborough, Leicestershire, England

Printed in England

Billy Goats Gruff

by Fran Hunia
illustrated by John Dyke

Ladybird Books

Here are
the billy goats Gruff.

This is
little billy goat Gruff.

He likes to jump.

This is
middle-sized
billy goat Gruff.

He likes
to have fun.

This is
big billy goat Gruff.

He likes
to eat grass.

Here is a bridge.

A big troll lives
under the bridge.

12

13

The billy goats Gruff
want to go
over the bridge
for some grass.

Trip, trap,
trip, trap, trip, trap.

Little billy goat Gruff
is on the bridge.

Up jumps the troll.

He says,
"I want
to eat you up."

"No, no," says
little billy goat Gruff.

"Here comes
middle-sized
billy goat Gruff.

He is big and fat.

You can
eat **him**
up!"

"Yes," says the troll.
"Yes, I can."

"I can eat
middle-sized
billy goat Gruff,"
says the troll.
"You can go
over the bridge."

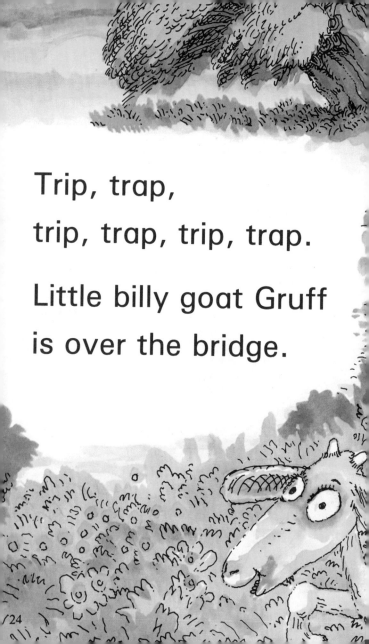

Trip, trap,
trip, trap, trip, trap.

Little billy goat Gruff
is over the bridge.

Middle-sized
billy goat Gruff
looks up.

"Little billy goat Gruff
is over the bridge,"
he says.

"He has some grass
to eat.

I can go
over the bridge
for some grass."

Trip, trap,
trip, trap, trip, trap.

Middle-sized
billy goat Gruff
is on the bridge.

29

Up jumps the troll.

He says, ''I want
to eat you up.''

"No, no," says
middle-sized
billy goat Gruff.

"Here comes
big billy goat Gruff.

He is big and fat.

You can
eat **him** up."

"Yes," says the troll.

"I can eat
big billy goat Gruff.

You can go
over the bridge."

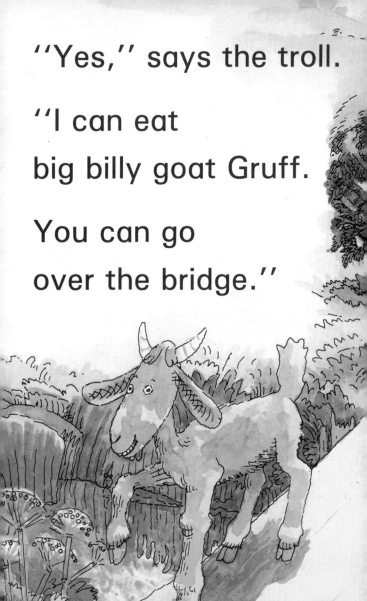

Trip, trap,
trip, trap, trip, trap.

Middle-sized
billy goat Gruff
is over the bridge.

Big billy goat Gruff
looks up.

"Little billy goat Gruff
and middle-sized
billy goat Gruff
are over the bridge,"
he says.

"I can go
over the bridge
for some grass."

Trip, trap,
trip, trap, trip, trap.

Big billy goat Gruff
is on the bridge.

Up jumps the troll.

He says,
"I want to eat
you up."

"No, no," says
big billy goat Gruff.
"I want to eat
you up."

Up goes the troll.

He goes

SPLASH

into the water.

Trip, trap,
trip, trap, trip, trap.

Big billy goat Gruff
is over the bridge.

The billy goats Gruff
have fun in the grass.

They eat and eat
and eat.

"We like it here,"
they say.